Amara's Farm

To Kendon and the Kurzer family for
introducing me to your inspirational garden.
—J. B. -W.

For my Grandparents x.
—S. H.

Published by
PEACHTREE PUBLISHING COMPANY INC.
1700 Chattahoochee Avenue
Atlanta, Georgia 30318-2112
PeachtreeBooks.com

The illustrations were
created in Photoshop using
layers of hand painted ink and
watercolor textures.

Printed in December 2021 by Leo Paper Group in China
10 9 8 7 6 5 4 3 2

ISBN: 978-1-68263-165-2

Cataloging-in-Publication Data is available from the
Library of Congress

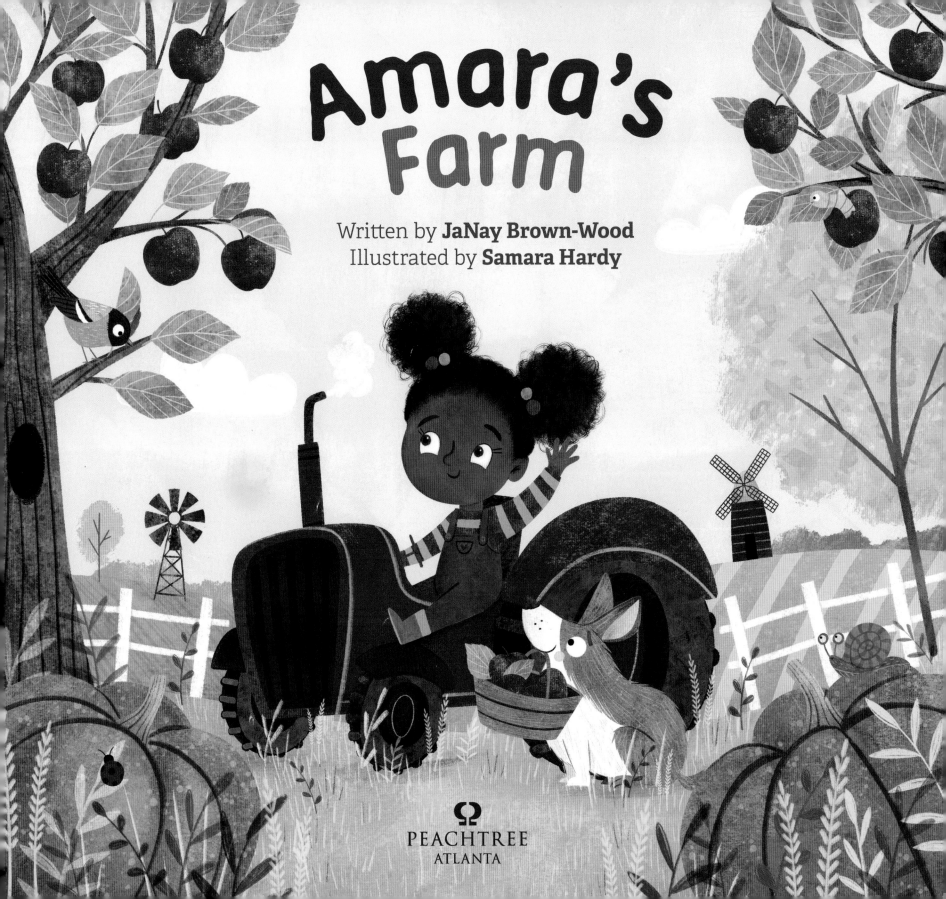

Amara's Farm

Written by **JaNay Brown-Wood**

Illustrated by **Samara Hardy**

PEACHTREE

ATLANTA

Amara has many plants on her farm.

Today, Amara must find her **pumpkins** for her autumn potluck. What do we know about **pumpkins**?

A pumpkin...

is large and round,
often orange,
and has a thick shell.

It grows on vines
and has a hard stem at the top.
And its mostly hollow center has...

orange pulp,
squishy innards,
and many seeds.

Let's help Amara find her pumpkins!

A **pumpkin** is large and round.
Is that a **pumpkin**?

No. That's an apple. An apple is round, but not large like a pumpkin.

A **pumpkin** is often orange
with lined ribs. Is that a **pumpkin**?

No. That's a persimmon. A persimmon
is orange, but it has a smooth,
waxy skin and no ribs.

A pumpkin has a thick and solid shell.
Is that a pumpkin?

No. That's a potato. A potato is solid, but
it has thin skin instead of a thick shell.

A **pumpkin** grows on the ground,
among leaves, and along a vine.
Is that a **pumpkin**?

No. That's cauliflower. Cauliflower grows on the ground, but it sprouts from the middle of its leaves and not along a vine.

A **pumpkin** has a hard stem that pokes upward from the top of its shell. Is that a **pumpkin**?

No. That's an eggplant. Eggplant stems poke upward, but they also have leafy bottoms that hang downward.

A pumpkin has one, mostly hollow, center. Is that a pumpkin?

No. That's okra. Okra is hollow, but it has many hollow spots throughout—not one large opening in the middle.

A **pumpkin** has firm, orange pulp.
Is that a **pumpkin**?

No. That's a kumquat. Kumquat pulp is
orange, but it's juicy and soft and not firm.

A **pumpkin** has squishy innards with long, stringy fibers. Is that a **pumpkin**?

No. That's a fig. A fig does have squishy innards, but no long, stringy fibers.

A **pumpkin** has many seeds with
white shells. Is that a **pumpkin**?

No. That's a kiwi. A kiwi has many seeds,
but kiwi seeds are black and not white.

Amara's potluck won't be complete
without her **pumpkins**.

We've searched and searched and still no luck!
Where, where, *where* can they be?

Are those **pumpkins?**

Why, yes! Those are **pumpkins!**

They are large, round, and orange with thick shells. They grow along a vine and have hard stems that poke upward. And they each have a hollow center, orange pulp, squishy innards, and many seeds.

Hooray! We've found Amara's pumpkins...

And just in time for some bountiful snacks!

Which produce can *you* find at Amara's potluck?

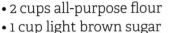

Molasses Pumpkin Bread
1 loaf (16 slices)

Ingredients

- 2 cups all-purpose flour
- 1 cup light brown sugar
- 1/2 tsp baking powder
- 1 tsp baking soda
- 1 tsp sea salt
- 1 1/2 tsp ground cinnamon
- 3/4 tsp ground nutmeg

- 1/4 tsp pumpkin pie spice (or ground cloves)
- 2/3 cup raisins
- 1/2 cup chopped walnuts [optional]
- 1/2 cup semi-sweet chocolate chips [optional]

- 2 large eggs
- 1/2 cup molasses
- 1 cup canned pumpkin
- 1/2 cup canola oil
- 1 tsp vanilla extract
- 1/2 cup water
- Cooking spray

Directions

1. With adult helper's aid, gather ingredients and cooking utensils.
2. Have adult helper preheat oven to 350°.
3. Grease one 9 x 5-inch loaf pan with cooking spray.
4. In large bowl, mix together all-purpose flour and brown sugar, breaking up sugar clumps.
5. Add baking powder, baking soda, sea salt, cinnamon, nutmeg, and pumpkin pie spice. Mix until blended, then stir in raisins. Set aside.
6. Have adult helper crack eggs and add to a separate medium-sized bowl.
7. Beat eggs with a whisk.
8. Add molasses, canned pumpkin, canola oil, vanilla, and water to eggs. Whisk together.
9. Stir egg mixture into the large bowl with the dry ingredients until moistened.
10. With adult helper's aid, pour mixture evenly into baking pan.
11. Evenly sprinkle chopped nuts and chocolate chips over the top of the mixture.
12. Bake for 45–60 minutes, until a toothpick inserted in center comes out clean.
13. Have adult helper remove hot pan while using oven mitts.
14. Cool in pan 10 minutes before removing to a wire rack.
15. Enjoy!

You'll also need: 1 trusty adult helper

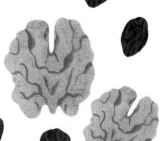

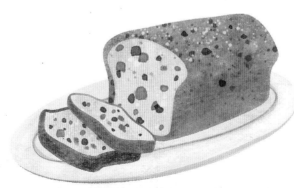